For all members of The Writers' Loft.
And most important, Heather Kelly, Founder & Empress. —J.F.

Shelley and Allan. Thanks for letting me raid the fridge when I visit! —B.K.

STERLING CHILDREN'S BOOKS
New York

An Imprint of Sterling Publishing
1166 Avenue of the Americas
New York, NY 10036

ISBN 978-1-4549-1960-5

Distributed in Canada by Sterling Publishing Co., Inc.
c/o Canadian Manda Group, 664 Annette Street
Toronto, Ontario, Canada M6S 2C8
Distributed in the United Kingdom by GMC Distribution Services
Castle Place, 166 High Street, Lewes, East Sussex, England BN7 1XU
Distributed in Australia by NewSouth Books
45 Beach Street, Coogee, NSW 2034, Australia

For information about custom editions, special sales, and premium and
corporate purchases, please contact Sterling Special Sales at 800-805-5489
or specialsales@sterlingpublishing.com.

Manufactured in China

Lot #:
2 4 6 8 10 9 7 5 3 1
05/17

www.sterlingpublishing.com

The artwork for this book was created using pencils and digital media.
Designed by Jo Obarowski and Ryan Thomann

Lady Pancake

SIR FRENCH TOAST

THE CASE

•••••• OF THE ••••••

Stinky Stench

by JOSH FUNK   illustrated by BRENDAN KEARNEY

STERLING CHILDREN'S BOOKS
New York

Back in the kitchen and deep in the fridge,
past Trifle Tower, across Taco Bridge,
on a vacation at Marshmallow Coast,
sat Lady Pancake beside Sir French Toast.

Knocking down syrup (from Northern Vermont),
over the bridge came Inspector Croissant.

"Uncle," Croissant said, "the fridge is in trouble!
A horrible stench turned a whole shelf to rubble!
I'm the last hope, or the fridge will be lost!
Help me, or else we'll be cooked, served, and sauced."

Nefarious odors began wafting by
as French Toast replied, "I will certainly try."

"I've got to succeed," said Croissant with a sob.
"I've solved zero cases since getting this job."

"It's Baron von Waffle, that devious square!"
said Pancake with anger. "Let's head to his lair!"

They started their search crossing Salsa Ravine,

And lumbered through smog around Mount Everbean.

Slowly they crept to the Onion Ring Cave.
"Baron Von Waffle," said Toast, "you old knave!"

"What are you doing here?" Waffle said, sneering.
"I'm sleuthing," Croissant said. "And you're interfering.
What do you know about smells that are vicious?"
"Nothing!" said Waffle. "My home smells delicious."

"Nephew," said Toast. "Waffle's right. It smells splendid."
The trio trudged out, but the case hadn't ended.

"The smell's getting worse," said Croissant with a shiver
as tater tots stumbled through Applesauce River.

An okra popped out of a red curry dish
and said, "There's a tale of a stinky red fish
who lurks at the bottom of Corn Chowder Lake."

"Great!" said Croissant as he tripped by Miss Steak.

Rowing their fastest with carrot-stick oars,
they studied the depths and they scanned all the shores.

"Ahoy!" cried Croissant. "A red herring! Right there!"
At last they'd unravel this stinky affair.

They paddled on forward, but as the boat neared,
a flavorful smoky aroma appeared.

It seemed the red herring was just a bad clue.
Dejected, the three didn't know what to do.

"It's time to give up," Pancake said with remorse.
"No!" said Croissant. "I'll discover the source!"

Inspector Croissant took a mighty big whiff.
"The odor is coming from Casserole Cliff!"

Peppers lay slumping and apples were dented.
Plums shrank to prunes and the beans had fermented.
That's when they saw it, the source of their woe . . .

. . . a moldy old fruitcake from eight months ago!

"Someone destroy him!" said Pancake. "Right now."
"Sure," replied Toast, "but I can't fathom how."

The fruitcake just cowered alone looking scared.
"Life isn't all bowls of cherries," he shared.

"I entered the fridge,

but then soon was forgotten.

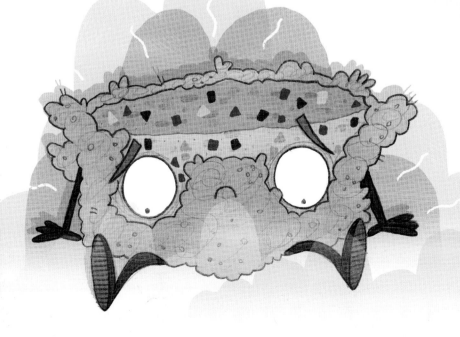

Slowly I crumbled, and
now I'm just rotten."

"This is my case," said Croissant. "I'll prevail.
Everyone knows fruitcakes never go stale.
How would you like being left to decay?
This is no villain. Let's help him. Make way!"

Together they journeyed past cliff, lake, and cave,
and offered the fruitcake a shower and shave.

Soon the old fruitcake was fresh as could be.
"What's that delectable smell?" asked Miss Brie.

With all nasty odors destroyed and dissolved,
the team celebrated and shouted, "Case solved!"